Dedicated To Kay Sullivan

True Love In Vermont
"Book Two"

By
Dorothea Zsenai Mongulla

Sheridan Books
Michigan

3

Copyright© 2007 by Dorothea Zsenai Mongulla

ISBN 978-1-60461-143-4

Manufactured in the United States of America
The people and places below are used in a fictitious manner to complete this fictitious work.

1. Snow Talbot-fictitious person
2. Emily Langdon-fictitious person
3. Kevin–fictitious person
4 Harry Frost/ Robert Andrews-fictitious person
5. Allan Postly-fictitious person
6. Nana/Vivian Stickler-fictitious person
7. Kate-fictitious person
8. Lee Ann-fictitious person
9. Madeleine-fictitious person
10. Maria von Trapp/Captain-fictitious persons
11. Julie Andrews-fictitious person
12. Christopher Plummer-fictitious person
13. Johannes von Trapp-fictitious person
14. Rusty Nail bar and grille-fictitious business
15. Bennington, VT-fictitious place
16. Stowe, VT-fictitious place
17. Peak Mill-fictitious business

18. Dwight Peter Stickler-fictitious person
19. David Reeves-fictitious person
20. Ben & Jerry's-fictitious business
21. Ferro Jewelers-fictitious business
22. NT Ferro-fictitious business
23. Bryan Ferro-fictitious person
24. The Charleston House-fictitious business
25. Katherine-fictitious person
26. Deana Jillson-fictitious person
27. Salon del sol-fictitious business
28. Wm Winand Chocolatier-fictitious business
29. Barbara Chamberlin-fictitious house cleaner
30. Willa & Dixi-fictitious persons
31. Adam & Alexandra-fictitious persons
31. The Parker House-fictitious business
32. Woodstock Inn-fictitious business
33. Linda Spellman-fictitious person

CHAPTER ONE

It was December 2nd, and the first snow of the season was covering the ground and trees. As Snow sat in her favorite chair with a cold glass of white wine in her hand, she slowly reflected on the past year.

Kevin, her new husband, was in the kitchen making a special pasta dish while Snow sat in front of a large crackling fire in the fireplace. She looked at the fire, then out through their large picture window at the snow coming down. She then glanced down at her engagement ring, which was shaped like a snowflake. The **snowflake**, thought Snow, starts out as a speck too small to see, with tiny bits of water attaching miraculously, creating six branches. Always hexagonal, no two flakes alike. *
No two lives alike, thought Snow.

Three years ago she was living in Westport, CT with her husband Richard. Widowed thereafter, she moved to Woodstock and opened a Real Estate office. She met Emily, who became her best friend. Together they searched for True Love. Snow found it and Emily was still looking.

*Information from Internet on Wilson Snowflake Bentley who dedicated his life to the study and photography of snowflakes.

Emily was very close to finding that **magic** when she met Allan Postly. All four of them, Snow, Kevin, Emily and Allan had so much fun together.

Finding out that Allan murdered his wife , and then killed himself, really gave them a scare. Snow could still remember the day the Detective returned to tell them the whole story. Allan had married four wealthy women, three of whom were still missing. Only one was found, the one he buried in Emily's backyard. Allan's wife Elizabeth, stopped haunting Emily and life was finally back to normal. **Whatever normal is!**

What a year! Thought Snow.

Just then Kevin walked into the room. "Need more wine Darling?" Kevin leaned down and kissed Snow on her forehead, then filled her glass.

"Kevin," said Snow, "thank you for being so wonderful." Kevin looked back at Snow. "You bring the best out of me." Snow smiled at Kevin. "It smells so good, when are we eating?" "Soon," answered Kevin, "you're going to love it!"

Snow was madly in love with Kevin. Together they had magic. Kevin had been there for her and Emily through thick and thin. He had helped Emily be a little more "approachable" to the opposite sex. A work that was still in progress, and soon he would be giving her ski lessons as well.

Kevin told Emily if she wanted to meet a skier, she should learn how to ski.

The three of them continued to go out in search of the perfect man for Emily. Since Allan's death, Emily seemed to take life a little less seriously. She still asked men if they were married or in marriage counseling, but now at least she introduced herself first.

Snow and Kevin continued to have a lot of laughs watching Emily talk to men. Slowly but surely she was improving on her "meeting men" skills.

It was very reassuring for Emily, knowing that Snow and Kevin were right there with her, while she was talking to strangers.

The three of them had grown closer since Allan's death. Emily had now become a best friend to Kevin as well.

But at the end of the night, Snow would turn to Kevin with a disparaging look and say, "Where is Emily's **"Knight in Shining Armor"**? Even **I** am getting impatient!"

Kevin would look back at Snow. "It's like you've always said Darling, perfect timing, it will happen. Don't be discouraged."

CHAPTER TWO

Emily drove into her driveway, stepped out of her car and walked into her house. It was Thursday, just one more work day until the weekend.

After putting on her comfy clothes, Emily headed into the kitchen to make dinner. Just then the doorbell rang. Emily jumped.

As she looked out the window, she saw an older woman holding a grocery bag. As Emily opened the door without concern, the woman started chatting.

"Hi, I'm your neighbor. I heard about the horrible things that have happened to you since you moved in. I feel terrible about not visiting you sooner. Years ago people brought their new neighbors apple pie. Nowadays most of us don't even know who our neighbors are."

"Please come in," said Emily.
"I hope this isn't a bad time to stop by," said the neighbor. "Oh no," said Emily, "I was just about to start dinner and have a drink."

The woman looked at Emily with a bright smile. "That's what's in my bag , I made us a large pitcher of Apple Martinis."

"With what you've been through, I thought you could use a drink." Emily laughed. "My name is Emily Langdon."

The older woman looked at Emily. "My name is Vivian Stickler, but everyone calls me Nana." Emily laughed again.

"So you live in the house next door?" asked Emily. "Yes," answered Nana, "the first one on the left out your driveway."

While having their first drink together, Emily started dinner. Nana made a toast to Emily, "To better days ahead." Emily really liked Nana. She was a fun person and very likeable.

Nana told Emily that she played golf, tennis and even skied. Emily looked back at Nana with a raised eyebrow.

"What?" asked Nana, "you're surprised? I'm 75, I'm not dead! Listen dear, Quechee was just voted "One of America's 100 Best Master Planned communities."* "It's a happening place here," said Nana, "and besides, I'm only 24 years older than you!"

*Article from Vermont Standard Newspaper.

16

"**Great**," said Emily, "I'm going to be **75** in 24 years? Pour me another drink!"
Nana laughed. "What's a nice girl like you doing, not being married?"

"I haven't found Mr. Right," said Emily, "I want the **magic**." "You should meet my son," said Nana, "you'd make a nice looking couple."

Emily replied, "Is he married?" "No dear," said Nana, "just engaged, and to a horrible girl. He was married. His wife died six years ago." "Oh, how terrible," responded Emily, "I'm so sorry. It must have been a difficult time. But either way, Nana, he's not free for me. I only date available men, not married, and not engaged."

"Well, that's your problem dear," said Nana. "What do you mean?" asked Emily. "Dear," said Vivian, "any man that isn't taken, couldn't be a good catch, or someone else would have already caught him. No wonder you're not married. When you meet Mr. Right, the universe has brought you together. You can't ignore it, or walk away. Do you have any idea how many couples are married to the wrong people? I'm not saying you should pursue married men, I'm just saying, that when you do meet your soul mate, you better not let him go."

"But Nana," answered Emily, "I have to be honest and upfront. I won't get involved with someone who is already in a relationship." Nana poured another Martini for herself. "I can see my work is cut out with you, **you really do need me!**"

"Let me tell you a story," said Nana, "I've been married 4 times." Emily was in shock. "Four times?"

"Yes," said Nana, "and all four are dead." "Nana," said Emily, "you've got to tell me everything, but first pour me another drink." Nana smiled.

Nana went on to tell Emily the story of all four marriages. She was one of four girls. Her older sister was going out with a very handsome man named Robert. When her sister broke up with him, he asked Nana on a date. They fell in love and married soon after. Robert was called to war and killed a month later. Meanwhile Nana found out she was pregnant with his child. She had to move back in with her mother.

It was a very difficult time. About a year later, a wonderful man came into her life. "Back then," said Nana, "I was beautiful, you'd never know it now. I didn't love him, but he loved me. My True Love was my first husband. Times were different back then. I hadn't gone to college so I needed support. My second husband was financially secure, and that is what my son and I needed, security."

Emily interrupted Nana. "I could never marry for money, it has to be for Love."

Nana continued to tell her story. "My second husband had a heart attack 5 years later, leaving me a wealthy widow."

"About 2 years after that, I met the most wonderful man. He was so handsome and how he made me laugh. He was a traveling salesman, always flying somewhere."

"Did you love him?" asked Emily. "In many ways I did," answered Nana, "He was a wonderful father to my son." Nana continued her story. "He went to work one day and never came home."
"What?" asked Emily.

"He never came home," said Vivian. "I was very close to his family. They never saw him again either. To this day, I don't know what happened to him."

"About 3 years later I met a very kind man at church. He was funny and I was lonely. Back then decent women didn't hang out in bars."

Emily laughed to herself, thinking how times have changed.

Nana went on to explain that she was married to him the longest, twenty years. "We had many good times together. One day I came home from shopping and he was lying on the floor. He had a stroke and died a week later."

"Oh, my gosh," said Emily, **"you should write a book."**

"Who'd believe it?" asked Nana. They both laughed.

Emily then told Nana what happened to her when she was ten years old. "My Dad was a pilot for a commercial airline."

"One day it was icy and rainy. He told the
airline it was too dangerous to take off.
The airline told him, you go up or you'll be
fired. So he went up. The plane crashed and
there was only one survivor, not my Dad.
The survivor wrote a book about the crash.
My Mom later found out that he had another
wife and family in another state. But my
mother still loved him anyway."

"You poor dear," said Nana, "I guess you
haven't had it easy either. What was your
father's name?" Emily looked at Nana,
"His name was Daddy."

In that moment, as Emily and Nana looked
at each other, a special bond was made.
From that day on they were close friends.

Their friendship was ageless. It was as if
they were two college girls. Just about
every night they had cocktails and dinner.
Nana didn't know how to boil an egg and
Emily knew master chef recipes by heart.

It was a healthy relationship for both of
them. They laughed and shared endless
stories.

Emily shared everything with Nana, including her friendship with Snow.

Now that Snow was married, Emily didn't see her as much as she used to, although they were still best friends.

CHAPTER THREE

Emily invited Snow and Kevin over for dinner to meet Nana. They all had a lot of laughs. Snow was fascinated with Nana's story of her four husbands.

Snow and Kevin embraced their new friendship with Vivian. When Snow invited Emily for dinner, Nana was also included.

Kevin gave Emily ski lessons and soon she became a fairly good skier. She and Kevin became closer friends through the process, with a whole new respect for each other.

Emily had subscribed to three online dating sites. Her online name was "Snowgirl". She never saw anyone she liked, and rarely got matches.

One morning while checking her email, Emily noticed a response from one of her dating sites. A very cute guy had sent her a message. His online name was "Smokey".

Emily brought up his info and found herself interested. In his bio he wrote that he was an honest person who doesn't play games. He had been married when he was younger but after a year, they knew they weren't right for each other.

Since then he had been searching for an honest and open woman, seeking a sincere relationship. In his section on likes and dislikes, Emily noticed one of his favorite books was one she read last summer.

Emily answered his response and from that point on, their emails to each other were on a daily basis.

When Snow heard about Ebe's (Snow's nick name for Emily) new adventure, she was happy for her but a little leery.

"Take it nice and slow," said Snow.
Emily replied, "That's easy for you to say, Missy, you found your TRUE LOVE! Times a wasting, I'm not getting any younger."

"You're right," said Snow, "but I care about you."

"I know," said Emily, "just care a little less for now, I need a man."

"Emily," said Snow, "Kevin has to go on a business trip next weekend. One of my clients has a time share at the "Trapp Family Lodge" in Stowe.

"Next weekend starts their week, but they have other plans, so they asked me if I wanted to go. Do you want to go with me, just for the weekend? You'll get to meet all new men."

"That sounds great," said Emily, "maybe I'll tell Smokey to meet us at the "Rusty Nail" for drinks. By the way, Snow, I forgot to tell you, I wrote on my bio that I live at Stowe. I thought that would protect me from stalkers."

"Very good," said Snow, "that was smart thinking."

CHAPTER FOUR

The week flew by. Snow and Emily were finally on their way to Stowe.

The night before, six inches of fresh snow fell all over the mountainsides. As they drove up Route 89 North, they noticed snow covered cabins on the hillsides with smoke coming out of their chimneys. It looked like a Currier & Ives picture.

"We are so blessed to be living in Vermont." Emily turned and smiled at Snow. *"We must have done something good."*

"That was the line in the song Julie Andrews sang to the Captain in *The Sound of Music*, as they danced in the gazebo." Snow sang the song to Emily, *"Somewhere in my youth or childhood, I must have done something good."* We must have been **very good** to be in Vermont."

"We were snow angels," said Emily, "remember when we made snow angels and nearly got concussions?" Snow laughed.

"That was the first time, I ever saw **real** powder snow."

"Is Maria von Trapp still alive?" asked
Emily. "No," answered Snow, "She and the
Captain died."

"That's sad," said Emily.

"Yes it is," responded Snow.
"I read that Maria was born in 1905, so that
would make her 102 if she were still alive.
I also read that Maria **wasn't** sent to the
Captain to be a governess, but to take care of
one of his daughters who had rheumatic
fever. She then married the Captain in
1927."*

"They opened the Lodge at Stowe in 1950.
It's a 2,400-acre resort and Johannes von
Trapp opened the first cross-country ski
center in Stowe."*

"Did you know that Vermont has more than
220 mountains with 18 ski resorts?"

"Wow," said Emily, "I knew we had a lot of
mountains, but not that many." Just then,
she and Emily simultaneously started
singing, *"away in the hills"*......

*Information from Internet and Trapp Family Lodge website.

<u>CHAPTER FIVE</u>

Snow and Emily got off Route 89 at Exit 10.
They turned right onto Route 100 North.
Just up the street was *"Ben & Jerry's"*, so
they stopped in to buy ice cream cones.

They continued on Route 100 North and
soon Emily shouted, "Take that left,
Moscow Road , it's a shortcut."

As they pulled up to the Trapp Family
Lodge, they were in awe as they looked out
to the marvelous views.

After unpacking their luggage they walked
over to the Austrian Tea Room for lunch.
The waitresses were dressed in traditional
Austrian attire. Between looking out the
large picture windows of mountainous views
and watching the waitresses, Emily and
Snow felt as if they were in Austria.

Madeleine, their waitress, brought Snow and
Emily a Rueben on marble rye. It was
delicious! After lunch they bought some
souvenirs, and then headed up the street for
a Horse Drawn Sleigh Ride.

When they got back from the Sleigh Ride
they went over to the Health & Fitness
Center for a massage. The good life!

CHAPTER SIX

At 6:30, Snow and Emily headed down the hill to *"the Rusty Nail bar & grille"*.

It was hard to find a parking place because the bar was packed.

"Do you think Smokey is here yet?" asked Emily. "Probably," answered Snow, "will you recognize him if you see him?"

"I printed out his picture," said Emily.

They entered the bar and were shocked at how many people were there. There was a large 20 foot screen over the dance floor.

Snow and Emily worked their way over to the bar and ordered two white wines. "Wow," said Emily, "this place rocks."

About ten minutes later, a fairly good-looking man found his way over to them. Emily turned her head and recognized him instantly. "Hi, Smokey," said Emily, "this is my friend Snow."

"I thought you were coming by yourself," said Smokey. "I changed my mind," answered Emily. "Hi, nice to meet you,"

said Snow, "Do you have a real name?"
"Yes," answered Smokey, "Harry Frost."

Snow laughed but Harry didn't. "I'm sorry
Harry," said Snow, "I wasn't laughing at
you. I was just thinking how funny it would
be if my last name was Frost, then my name
would be Snow Frost."

Harry half smiled at Snow. Emily was
speechless.

"May I buy you a beer, Harry?" asked
Snow. Finally Harry smiled brightly. Just
then, 3 seats were open at the bar, so they
grabbed them quickly. Harry sat between
Emily and Snow.

Emily was silent, so Snow tried to stir up a
conversation by asking Harry where he was
from.

"I'm from Bennington, Vermont."
"Oh," said Snow, "I've been to Bennington
many times."

"I love the Bennington Battle Monument
and gift shop, and the new lighting on the
Monument looks great."

"I've been to the Bennington Museum and saw the collection of Grandma Moses paintings. Wasn't she 75 years old when she started painting?"

Harry looked at Snow with amusement. "No, she was 76."

Snow smiled and continued sharing her knowledge of Bennington. "Oh, the covered bridges, I drove to all five of them. And Robert Frost's grave. I almost forgot. It's right there behind the "Old First Church". I love that fence around the graveyard.* What is that saying on Robert Frost's grave? "A lover's quarrel with the…?"

Harry replied, *"I had a lover's quarrel with the world."**

"Yes, yes, that's it. I also went to Robert Frost's house down the road there. Harry, are you related to him? " "No relation," answered Harry.

Just then Snow noticed Emily looking over toward them. She felt very bad all of a sudden. This was Emily's date and she was hogging him.

*Information found on Internet.

41

Snow then blurted out, without thinking, "Are you married or in marriage counseling, Harry?" "No," he answered.

Emily started laughing out loud and then Snow laughed with her.

Emily looked at Harry. "I'm sorry, **my friend is being unapproachable**, and you'll have to excuse her."

Snow gave Emily a look, but couldn't be mad, since it was true. What happened? thought Snow. Have we reversed roles? Usually it's Emily who asks these questions.

As Snow looked back at Emily, she saw her laughing with Harry. They were talking and actually looked like they were having a good time.

Snow went outside to call Kevin on her cell. He'll never believe this, thought Snow.

About fifteen minutes later, Snow walked back into the bar. Emily was sitting alone. "Where's Harry?" asked Snow. "He went to the bathroom."

"Oh, good," said Snow, "I thought I scared him off. And by the way Emily, I'm so sorry. I don't know what got into me. He's your date and I went on and on. I'm sorry, please forgive me." "It's ok," said Ebe, "it was sort of funny, especially when you asked him if he was married." They both laughed.

"Well," said Snow, "it was very rude of me and I'm sorry. You know **me** and history. Once I start, I can't stop. So, what do you think, do you like him?" Emily looked back at Snow and rolled her eyes.

"What?" asked Snow, "What's **the trouble with Harry**?"* "No **magic**," said Emily, "but he's nice. We actually have a lot in common." "Well, that's good," said Snow.

Just then Smokey came back. He appeared to be happy now. He was smiling and laughing. For about an hour, the three of them talked at the bar. A few times Emily even danced with him. Emily came back from the dance floor and went straight to the ladies room.

*"The Trouble With Harry", is the Title of the 1955 Alfred Hitchcock movie made partly in Stowe, Vermont.

While Emily was gone, Snow continued talking to Harry about Bennington.

As Emily walked out of the bathroom , a man walking past her bumped into her arm, emptying her purse onto the floor. There were so many people standing there, it was nearly impossible for Emily to pick it all up.

As she knelt on the floor, a man bent down to help her. Emily looked over to the stranger. Just then, as they looked at each other, there was **"MAGIC"**!

Emily gazed at the man while he continued to pick everything up. He then looked at her and smiled. "Hi, I'm Peter." Emily smiled back, but all she could say was, "Hello." This was **THE** moment she had waited for.

No, not spilling her purse on the floor, finding **the magic**. She had always dreamed about one day meeting a man and feeling the **magic**. That moment finally came and for some strange reason she couldn't speak, not even ask questions, like, are you married or are you in marriage counseling, nothing. She just smiled at him as she's never smiled before, and he smiled back.

Just then his friend yelled out, "Come on, let's go, I don't feel well." Peter reached over to Emily, gently touching her hand. "Are you alright?" Emily nodded yes and stood up. Peter got up and walked toward the door with his friend, but as he walked out the door, he turned back to see if Emily was still looking. She was. So he smiled and winked at her. Emily walked over to the door and opened it to see if she could still see him. She saw him get into a black Lexus with his friend and drive out of the parking lot.

Emily finally came back to reality and quickly walked over to Snow. Harry wasn't there. She told Snow the whole episode in less than a minute. Snow then told Emily, "Let's go see if we can find him."

They quickly got on their coats and headed out the door. They looked around to see where Harry was, but he was nowhere in sight.

Peter dropped off his friend at the Inn up the street. "Listen," said Peter to his friend, "I'm going back to the bar, to see if I can find that girl, I'll see you later."

Peter quickly turned around and headed back to the Rusty Nail. As he got closer, he saw cars turning in and out of the entrance. As he slowed down to turn in, he noticed Emily's face in the passenger side of a car pulling out. He was blocked by a car in front of him and in back. By the time he turned around, Emily was nowhere in sight.

Emily and Snow drove around for an hour. "Great," said Emily, "I finally meet Mr. Right and I don't even know his last name or phone number."

"Snow" said Emily, "I know this may sound crazy, but I just know **he's the one**."

"It's not crazy," responded Snow, "that's how TRUE LOVE is. You just know. Don't be upset either. Just as surely as you met him, somehow, you **will** see him again.

"Promise?" asked Emily. "Promise," answered Snow.

CHAPTER SEVEN

Emily tossed and turned all night.
The next morning after breakfast, they drove all over Stowe looking for a black Lexus.

They finally decided to head back home. Although they didn't find Peter, Emily was still hopeful.

"Wait till I tell Nana," said Emily, "she won't believe it."

"She'll be proud of you for trying to find him," said Snow.

The next day Emily wrote to Smokey telling him that she was sorry she left before saying goodbye. He didn't reply.

Nana was so excited for Emily when she heard the story. "I'm so proud of you, Emily," said Nana, "That was a big step for you. I know for sure, you will see him again."

That Friday night, Snow, Kevin and Emily decided to go to Killington. The Peak Mill was crowded. As they parked their car and walked in, they saw Harry sitting at the bar.

He turned as they approached the bar and smiled at Emily. "Hi, this is a nice surprise."

"Hi, Harry," said Emily, "Did you get my email?" "Yes," said Smokey, "Sorry, I've been busy."

"That's alright," said Emily, "I just wanted you to know I felt bad about leaving without saying goodbye."

Emily introduced Harry to Kevin. They seemed to hit it off right away, and spent most of the night talking "man talk".

Emily didn't see Peter and because of him, she had no desire to talk to other men that night.

They all left around 11pm. Harry's pickup truck was parked right next to them. They shared goodbyes and went home.

CHAPTER EIGHT

Monday morning Snow had a lot of errands
to do, one of which was going to her hair
dresser, Deana Jillson. Deana had just
opened her own salon, called "Salon del
sol". It's located by the blinking light on
Route 4, just east of the Taftsville Bridge.
Deana named her business after the Sun,
since she loved it so much. Snow told her,
"That was a BRIGHT idea!" Deana
laughed.

Snow enjoyed visiting with Deana while
getting her hair done. Snow always had her
do a foil and personally called her hair color,
"Home Wrecker Blonde".

Snow's next stop was the Hardware store,
where her friend Lee Ann worked. Snow
went in to get some light bulbs and garbage
bags.

"Hi, Snow," said Lee Ann.
"How are you doing?" asked Snow.
"Good," answered Lee Ann, "I've been
riding my horse, *Big*."

Just then a woman walking into the store
interrupted their conversation. The woman
walked over to the counter with some
posters in her hands.

"Excuse me, my name is Linda Spellman. My brother was hiking through Vermont and the last time I spoke to him, he was leaving Woodstock walking east on Route 4. I made these posters because I haven't heard from him since then. This is my sixth visit to this area trying to find him."

Snow and Lee Ann looked closely at the poster. "His disappearance was in the middle of July?" asked Snow.

"Yes," said Linda, "every summer my brother comes to Vermont to hike. He's always had the **safest** times. But this last time is a mystery to us, since he always stayed in touch."

Lee Ann took the poster and taped it on the door.

"I **never** heard of any hiker having problems in Vermont," said Snow. "**Me neither**," echoed Lee Ann.

Snow hurried back to work. At 12:30 she would be showing three properties to a couple she had shown properties to, on two other occasions.

This would be their third home. They lived on the Cape, had a Brownstone in Boston and wanted a Federal Style house in Woodstock.

"We have plenty of those," thought Snow. The village of Woodstock is filled with Federal style homes. Brick and clapboard houses with white picket fences, brass fixtures and perfectly manicured lawns.

Little shops along the sidewalks, with window boxes overflowing with flowers. It's a picture perfect town. It was voted the **"Prettiest Small Town in America"**.

CHAPTER NINE

Around 9:30 a.m., Nana went for her daily walk down the street past Emily's house, to the cul-de-sac and back home. As she passed Emily's house on her way back, she noticed a green pick up truck in Emily's driveway.

"Hmm," thought Vivian, "I don't remember Emily saying anyone was going to be at her house."

When Nana got inside her house, she sat by the front window, watching for the truck to leave. About 20 minutes went by, and still no truck, so Nana decided to walk over to Emily's house.

She brought a pen and paper with her to write down the license plate number. As she walked out of her driveway and onto the road, the truck was backing out of Emily's driveway.

Nana inconspicuously looked at the driver and license plate number. Nana didn't want to cause suspicion, so she continued to walk. Once the truck was out of sight, Nana went back to her house. She decided to call the Detective who was in charge of the case with Allan Postly. She didn't want to alarm Emily, so she called the Detective herself.

As she was calling the police, she saw the green truck drive past her house, heading back toward Emily's. The truck was moving very slowly and the driver was looking at Nana's house very carefully.

When Nana saw him look at her house, she backed up so he couldn't see her standing by the window. "Now, that is very strange," thought Nana. "Why is he looking at my house? Maybe he thought I was going to spy on him and he wanted to see if I was still walking." Either way, Nana felt very nervous.

Within 3 minutes the truck headed back out of the road. Nana was on hold with the police department. "Yes," said Nana, "this is Vivian Stickler, I'm Emily Langdon's neighbor over in Quechee."

The Detective took all the information and told Nana not to worry, "it could be a handyman doing some work at Emily's." He told her he would run a check on the license plate number, just to give her "peace of mind."

Nana felt a little better after talking with him, but she wasn't going to tell Emily. That poor girl had been through so much. Nana decided to be in charge. She felt she had to make it up to Emily, for not being there previously when she needed a good neighbor.

Nana wanted to walk back over to Emily's, but she was too afraid the truck might come back and see her there.

She decided to call Snow. After Nana explained everything, Snow told Vivian she and Kevin would be right over.

Kevin and Snow walked all around Emily's house, and then went inside to see if anything was noticeably different.

Nothing looked out of place, so they drove over to Nana's and went in to talk with her.

"Snow," said Nana, "the Detective just called back. He said the truck belongs to a Robert Andrews. He lives in Bennington. The Detective said he ran a check on him, he has no police record."

Snow looked at Kevin. "I don't know anyone by that name. Does that name ring a bell with you?"

Kevin looked back at Snow. "No, that name doesn't sound familiar, but Harry has a green pick up truck and he lives in Bennington."

CHAPTER TEN

Snow immediately phoned the Detective. He told them to come over to the police station.

The Detective agreed that too many coincidences aren't coincidences at all. He told them he would have a friend in the police force at Bennington go over to the address they got from the DMV.

The Detective also told them to tell Emily all that transpired, just in case he was a stalker.

Snow and Kevin forgot that it was Friday. They had promised Emily they would all go to Killington that night.

Nana, Snow and Kevin went over to Emily's house and started dinner, so that when she came home they could explain the latest happening.

When Emily pulled into her driveway, she was thrilled to see Snow and Kevin's car. As she walked inside her kitchen door, she saw all three of them looking at her.

"Is it my Birthday and I forgot?"

Snow and Nana walked over to Emily,

and kissed her on the cheek.

"Is it my funeral?" asked Emily.
"No dear," answered Nana, "Can't anyone surprise you without it being the end of the world?" Everyone laughed.

Emily got into her comfy clothes and had a glass of her favorite white wine, Meursault, which Snow and Kevin brought over.

Kevin had slow cooked barbeque ribs in the oven and made a large pot of fluffy white rice.

After dinner, Nana told Emily what had taken place. To everyone's surprise, Emily wasn't upset or concerned.

"Well," said Emily, "I'm glad you gave me my favorite wine first. I truly believe everything is going to be alright. I won't live being afraid of my own shadow. I love this house. This house and I have been through a lot together and we will survive."

"Since Allan, I have learned to face my fears, and in so doing, I have learned that *there is nothing to fear, but fear itself.*"

"When I heard those footsteps upstairs while lying in bed, the thought of what it might be was worse than actually seeing the Ghost. When I saw Elizabeth standing at the window, I was more shocked than scared."

"And on top of that, my friendship with the three of you has given me great strength. I'm a survivor, my Dad taught me that."

"By the way, you promised to take me to Killington tonight. I think we should still go and if we see Harry, or Robert, I won't be afraid. I think we should have one of the waitresses call out the name Robert, and see if he turns his head. If he does, then we'll know more than the police."

CHAPTER ELEVEN

Snow and Kevin told Nana and Emily to
stay with them at their home, until they
knew more, but both declined the offer.

Nana went home and the three of them went
to Killington. Harry wasn't there. They still
had a good time anyway. Emily looked for
Peter, thinking that if he was a skier,
he might be there also, but he wasn't.

While in the car on their way home, Emily
asked Snow if she and Kevin would go up
with her to the Rusty Nail at Stowe, the
following night.

"Maybe Peter will be there," said Emily.
Snow couldn't say no to Ebe. "Alright,"
said Snow, "maybe we'll see Peter and
Harry. It's only an hour away, but I'll get us
two rooms at the Trapp Family Lodge. We
had a great time there, and I'd love to eat at
the Austrian Tea Room again. Maybe we'll
drive up in the morning and take another
sleigh ride, this time all three of us."

Snow and Kevin dropped off Emily, once
again asking her to reconsider staying with
them. Emily reassured them she would be
fine.

When Snow and Kevin finally got home, Snow headed for the bathroom to take a hot shower.

Kevin heard Snow running the water and decided to join her. Snow was already in the shower by the time Kevin walked into the room.

He could see her naked body through the glass doors. He stood there looking at her silhouette. "How beautiful she was," he thought. He loved her so much. "They really were soul mates," he thought.

As Snow showered, Kevin opened the glass door. He walked in and pressed his body up against the back of Snow's wet body.

His manhood enlarged. He gently rested it against Snow's rear cheeks. Snow turned around and kissed Kevin passionately. He kissed her neck then placed his lips on her nipples. She moaned.

He gave each breast equal time, he didn't want the "*girls*" to be jealous. Snow forcefully grabbed Kevin toward him for another kiss. Snow loved kissing him.

Snow then kneeled on the shower floor,
placing her mouth on Kevin's sex spear.
With her whole mouth she gently but firmly
sucked him. Kevin moaned out loud.

Snow continued to suck and lick him, she
then licked his manhood grouping. Sounds
of ecstasy came from his lips. Snow slowly
stood up and kissed Kevin passionately.

Kevin lowered his head to Snow's love
mounds, licking them relentlessly.
His mouth then rose to hers, kissing her
once again.

Snow leaned back against the wall, holding
onto the stainless steel bar. She
rose her leg up, to let Kevin place his
manhood into her warm wet walls.

Kevin pushed his manhood in, moaning
loudly. Warm water was running down their
bodies. He pushed in and out of her in a
perfect rhythm. They moved simultaneously
back and forth. It was so warm and so wet.
It felt so good. Kevin continued at the same
speed, it was too good to change.

Snow's breasts rubbed against Kevin's
chest. It made her nipples hard.

Snow soon screamed out, and Kevin cried out right after. Snow put her leg back down and Kevin pressed up against her body, kissing her gently on the lips.

"I love you, my little mermaid."
Snow smiled back. "And I love you, my mighty pirate."

CHAPTER TWELVE

The next morning Snow and Kevin picked up Emily. They drove up Route 89 North to Stowe.

Emily told them she slept great and that nothing unusual had happened in the house. So in spite of the fact that a stranger had been at her house without her knowledge, it didn't appear to have been for any wrong doing.

As Kevin drove, Snow and Emily sang songs from the "*Sound of Music.*" Occasionally Kevin joined in.

"Doe a deer, a female deer....."

"Snowflakes on mittens........"

"Goodnight, farewell, aufiedersehn,"

They didn't quite get the wording right, but none the less, they had a lot of fun.

"What a wonderful family, the von Trapps'," said Snow, "I'm so glad they settled in Vermont. What a journey with those children, coming all the way from Austria to America."

"**It's still** the land of opportunity," said Kevin.

Snow told Kevin the story of Maria, the same story she told Emily.

As soon as they arrived, they unpacked and went for a sleigh ride. It was absolutely perfect. The sun was out, but snow was lightly falling. Snow sat in the middle with Kevin on her right and Emily on her left. They covered themselves with heavy wool blankets and sat as closely as possible.

Snow started singing some more "*Sound of Music*" songs. Kevin and Emily joined in. This time they sang loudly, laughing as they changed songs.

"We need Julie Andrews to help us sing. I wonder if she ever stayed here," questioned Emily.

"Wouldn't that have been something if Julie Andrews and Christopher Plummer were here at the same time?" asked Snow.

Kevin then said, "I'm sure they were at some point. After all, that was one of the greatest movies of all time."

"I also loved her in Mary Poppins," said Emily, "I was only eight years old then." They went to the Austrian Tea room for lunch, then down into town to shop at the local stores.

They went to the Rusty Nail at 6 pm, so that they could get three seats together at the bar. After 6:30 the place was too packed to find seats.

Emily didn't write to Smokey that week, so he had no idea they were at Stowe. They ordered drinks and Calamari.

Snow was talking to Kate, one of the waitresses she befriended on their previous visit. Snow asked her to call out the name Robert, if Harry shows up. They had it all planned. If he turns his head when she calls out the name, then she would quickly turn away, so that he wouldn't know she did it purposely.

It was a good plan, somewhat dangerous, but Kate was game. At 7:30, in walked Harry. He noticed Emily and the gang right away. As he walked over to Emily, he asked, "Why didn't you email me you were coming?"

Emily smiled and said, "We wanted to surprise you."

Just then Snow and Kevin turned around to say hello. Harry smiled back. He actually liked them. They got along well and had a lot of laughs.

As Harry looked at them, he thought to himself, **"It's going to be hard to kill Emily."**

They drank, ate and even danced. Pretty soon the moment was perfect for Kate to call out the name, Robert.

Harry was talking to Kevin, who was facing away from the bar. Kate went to the side of the bar and called out the name. She quickly turned her head as planned, pretending she was helping a customer at the bar.

Harry heard someone call the name Robert. Kate had said it loud enough and so unexpectedly, that Harry was caught off guard, and **did** turn his head.

Emily and Snow noticed his reaction but quickly said in unison, "Anyone care to dance?"

It worked, they thought. Harry had no clue.
He didn't act suspicious nor did he change
his demeanor.

In spite of the suspense and new revelation,
they continued to talk at the bar and actually
enjoyed the rest of the evening.

CHAPTER THIRTEEN

As Harry left the Rusty Nail, he couldn't help but feel bad about having to harm Emily.

He had no choice, he thought.

After all, it was **her fault** his brother was dead.

Allan and he had a bad childhood. Their father was an abuser. He had tormented their Mother to the point of pushing her down the stairs to her death.

Harry and Allan were there when it happened. Their father laughed when he saw there mother lying at the foot of the stairs.

Allan was 15 and Harry was only 13.

That was the night that changed their lives. Allan was so angry with his father for what he did to their mother that he charged after him while he was standing on the top step, causing him to fall down the stairs also.

Allan stood there, looking down at his dead parents. He turned to his brother Harry and said, "I killed him, you get rid of him."

Harry knew he wasn't strong enough to move his father, so he could only think of one thing to do, **burn the house down**.

Harry went into the garage and grabbed the gasoline can. He poured it all around the foundation of the house.

His brother watched while leaning against his father's pick up truck with a cigarette hanging out of his mouth.

Harry looked over to Allan.

"Do you want to light the match?"

Allan looked at Harry, shaking his head no.

Harry hesitated, but knew he had to finish the job. He lit the match and within five minutes the house was an inferno.

As Harry watched the flames engulf the house, he felt scared yet excited. Something deep within him liked it.

It was that night that Harry became an arsonist, and Allan a murderer.

Up until that point, they had been good boys, never in trouble. But something happens inside a person's mind once they decide to do something really bad. They start to believe they were never good, and from that point on act badly, believing they really are bad people.

For thirty seven years they had been on the run.

It was in Vermont that they found **some** solitude. Allan had settled in Quechee and Harry in Bennington. They knew enough to live apart, so that the police would find it harder to track them down.

That is why Harry wanted to kill Emily. He held her solely responsible for taking his brother's only happiness away. It was her fault his brother was dead. He would have to get rid of her, as he did with so many others, and how he knew best, with **fire.**

The only problem was that he liked them; Emily, Snow and Kevin, just as his brother did. They appealed to a side which had reminded them of happy times they shared with their mother. She was a good mother, and always made her boys laugh, hoping to compensate for their abusive father.

Allan had emailed Harry when he first started seeing Emily. He would share everything about Emily with him, even mentioning what books she read.

That's why Harry was able to find Emily on the internet dating site. Of course he had to use the name Smokey, any good arsonist would.

What Harry didn't expect, was liking her. Not as a girlfriend, but as a person. It made it difficult to kill her.

He had gone to her house to set a timer on her propane gas tank, but he couldn't do it. And on top of that, some nosey neighbor saw him in his truck.

That's when he had to ditch his truck and move out of his apartment. "It would have been easier to kill the old bitch," thought Harry. But he didn't want to draw attention to Emily's house before he burned it down.

CHAPTER FOURTEEN

When Emily got back home from Stowe, her answering machine had a message from Nana.

"Call me when you get home dear."

Emily called Nana. "Hi, I just walked in."

"Emily," said Nana, "you better come over, the Detective called. You'll want to sit down to hear this."

"Should I call Snow?" asked Emily.
"Yes dear," answered Nana. "I ordered a whole meal from the country club restaurant, so why don't you all come over for dinner."

While driving over to Nana's, Snow and Kevin wondered what on earth the Detective could have told her.

"It couldn't be good," said Kevin, "or she would have told Emily on the phone."

Snow turned and looked at Kevin.

After they arrived, Nana told them to eat first, then after dinner she would tell them what the Detective said.

After dinner they gathered in Nana's living room.

Snow noticed pictures of a little boy on all of the cocktail tables. "Is this your grandchild?"

"No dear," answered Nana, "that's my son Dwight, when he was a boy."

"How old is he now?" asked Snow.
"53," said Nana.

They all sat patiently, waiting for Vivian to share her information.

Nana looked at them and said, "I'm sorry to be the bearer of bad news, but you need to know what the Detective told me."

"He sent his friend on the police force in Bennington over to that guy's apartment. The apartment was empty except for a garbage can under the kitchen sink."

"He dumped it out and found some old newspaper clippings. The clippings were about Allan Postly's death."

Emily, Snow and Kevin were speechless.

"I'm sorry," said Nana.
"The Detective thinks Harry is in some way connected with Allan. He phoned Chicago to see if he could find out any more information on Allan's history. He thinks they're related."

"So what does that mean?" asked Snow, "Is Emily in danger?"

"Well," answered Nana, "quite possibly she is. Until the Detective calls us back with more information, we won't know one way or the other."

"You know…. now that I think about it," said Snow, "Harry and Allan have a lot of similar characteristics. They're both charming and they even have the same laugh."

"And Harry has the same eyes as Allan," said Emily, "I bet you they're brothers. That would explain why Harry said he read the same book I read. His brother probably told him."

Kevin interjected. "So the question is , why is Harry interested in us?"

"I doubt that it's for a good reason," said Snow.

They all looked sullenly at each other and nodded.

"Well," said Kevin, "I don't care how much you love your home Emily, you and Nana will be staying at our house until this mess is cleared up."

No one argued with him.

Nana stood up to go into the kitchen. As she started to walk, she fell on the floor. She started talking in a peculiar way. Her words were slurred.

They all started yelling, "Nana, Nana, are you all right?" But she wasn't.

Emily ran to the phone and called 911.

Snow looked at Nana and asked, "Are you a diabetic?" Nana nodded no.

"She is acting like she is in a diabetic insulin shock. My grandfather was a diabetic and I once saw him like this."

Snow ran to the refrigerator to get some orange juice. Supposedly it helps, if you are in a diabetic insulin shock. She found a quart and poured a little bit in a glass.

"Are you sure you should give that to her?" asked Emily. "Maybe she has something else, and having orange juice would be bad."

Snow looked at Emily. "You're right, but maybe a drop won't hurt."

Emily gently held Nana's head up on her lap, while Snow carefully placed the glass on Nana's lips. "Just a drop," said Emily.

By now they could hear an ambulance siren. They were relieved.

The EMT's rushed into the house and hovered over Nana. They did all kinds of things to her and asked her all kinds of questions.

About 15 minutes later, they told Emily, Snow and Kevin, "It looks as though she's

in insulin shock." They quickly rushed her
into the ambulance.

As they carried her out the door, Nana was
shouting, "c...c...c...all th...th...the boy."
"You mean Dwight?" asked Emily.
Nana nodded. "Where's his number?"
"B.b.bed...room," said Nana,
"r.r.red...book."

Emily ran into Nana's bedroom and saw a
red book on her night stand. She quickly
turned the pages to find Dwight's number.

It wasn't under his name. "Where is it?" she
thought. "Is it under "**the boy**"?"
Sure enough, it was.

Emily quickly dialed his cell number.
He answered. "Thank God," thought Emily.

Emily explained everything to him and told
him Nana was on her way to the Hospital.
He told her he was on his way and would
see her there.

Emily hung up the phone. As she turned to
leave the bedroom, she noticed a picture on
Nana's dresser. Emily stood in shock as she
looked at the man in the frame.

"Snow? Kevin?" called Emily, "Come in here right away."

Snow and Kevin ran into the bedroom. "Are you alright?" asked Snow.

Emily turned her head toward them and said, **"This is Peter. This is a picture of Peter."**

"What?" asked Snow, "What did you say?"

"This is Peter, this is Mr. Right. This is the guy from the Rusty Nail that helped me with my pocket book."

Kevin and Snow looked at the picture, then back at Emily. No one spoke.

CHAPTER FIFTEEN

Harry decided that no matter how much he liked Emily, out of allegiance to his brother, he had to kill her.

He drove over to Quechee with all the tools he needed to complete the job.

He slowly drove up Emily's street, glancing at the old ladies house on his way.

"Hmm," he thought, "looks like nobody's home."

He parked his car past Emily's driveway and walked back toward her house. It was dusk, so he could still see.

He walked into the backyard and peeked into the windows to see if Emily was home. There was no sign of anyone.

He sat on the patio contemplating what he should do. He thought he should burn down the house even though she wasn't home. "Maybe it's better not to kill her," he thought. "Maybe burn the bitch neighbor's house too! Two for one."

Just then he heard a noise. It was someone in the woods, walking directly toward him.

He froze, not knowing what to do. Within seconds a man stood directly in front of him.

"Hey Bro", said the man.

"You're alive, you're alive," shouted Harry, "I thought you were dead."

"No Bro," answered Allan, "I'm alive, but more importantly, **why are you here?**"

"I thought Emily was responsible for your death, so I decided to get even with her."

"Listen Harry," said Allan, "It was my fault, not hers. I never should have buried Elizabeth here. It was sloppy work. I'm getting lazy in my old age. And that wedding picture? I was a stupid ass for leaving it out."

"Why are you making excuses for her?" asked Harry.

"Quite simply," answered Allan, "I like **her**, I like **them**. They gave me the most normal life I've ever known. When I was with them, I wasn't Allan a murderer , I was Joe Schmo, a normal guy, living a normal life."

102

"How'd you know I was here?" asked Harry.

"I went to Bennington to see you, and your buddy John said you were headed to Quechee for some unfinished business. Unfinished business only means one thing to guys like us."

"Let's get out of here," said Allan, "Vermont is way too peaceful and the people are way too friendly for my liking." Harry laughed.

"Don't you think we could be good people again, like when we were kids?" asked Harry.

"Nice thought, Bro, but that's all it is. We went too far, too many times. We've spent more time being bad than good. I no longer know how to be good, and quite frankly, it seems boring."

Harry and Allan walked to their cars.

"Where should we go?" asked Harry.

"Somewhere warm, maybe Florida."

"Hey?" asked Harry, "if you didn't die, then who got smashed to bits at the bottom of the Gorge in your place?"

Allan smiled. "That, my brother, was a gift placed in my lap. I was headed out of Vermont, and as I drove over the Quechee Gorge, I noticed a hiker with a back pack. Sweet, I thought, so sweet!"

"I placed my wallet in his pocket and took his. He never knew what happened. I knocked him out and threw him over the railing."

CHAPTER SIXTEEN

"I was never in Nana's bedroom before," said Emily, "or I would have seen Peter's picture. Nana was right, her son would be perfect for me."

Snow and Emily laughed.

They got to the hospital within 20 minutes.

When they asked the nurse in the emergency room how Nana was, she asked if they were related. Emily looked at the nurse. "And if I said yes, how would you know if I really was or not?" "I'm sorry," replied the nurse, "this is hospital policy."

"And what if I told you I was her mother?" asked Emily. The nurse just looked at her. "Come on," said Snow, "The Boy is on his way, they'll tell him everything."

When Peter walked into the waiting room, he froze when he saw Emily. Emily looked up and smiled at him. He smiled back.

For at least 15 seconds neither one of them said a word.

Snow walked over to Peter. "Hi, I'm Snow, I'm a friend of your mothers, and this is my husband Kevin. Your mother always calls you Dwight."

"Oh, hello," said Peter, "my Mother has told me so much about you both. Yes, my name is Dwight, but I prefer my middle name, Peter."

Snow then said, "And this is my best friend Emily, your mother's neighbor."

Peter walked over to Emily. "I believe we've met before, at Stowe." Emily smiled and nodded. "I never thanked you for helping me that night."

Just then a Doctor walked over to them. "Is anyone here related to Vivian Stickler?"

"Yes," answered Peter, "she's my mother."

The Doctor talked to Peter in private. "Your mother is alright. It appears she is a diabetic. Her blood sugar levels were off. She was in insulin shock when she arrived at the hospital. She's fine now, but she will have to go on a special diet to control her sugar levels. I 'd like to keep her here overnight , just to keep an eye on her."

Peter went in to see his Mother. She was too tired to see anyone else.

When Peter walked back out to the waiting room, he told them the information the doctor had shared with him.

It was now 9:30 p.m. Snow asked Peter if he had eaten supper and if he was planning on staying at his mother's house overnight.

He looked at Emily and said, "I stopped on the highway for a sandwich, but I sure could use a drink."

Snow suggested they go to a local restaurant.

After relaxing at the restaurant and having a glass of wine, Peter started talking about meeting Emily at Stowe.

He told them he went back to the Rusty Nail that night, but he passed them driving out of the parking lot.

Emily thought to herself, "He went back to the bar to see me? He really does like me."

CHAPTER SEVENTEEN

Peter stayed overnight at his mother's house. Emily decided to take off from work the next two days. This was tax season but between Nana being in the hospital and finding Peter, she couldn't go to work.

Emily had just passed the last part of her CPA exam of which there are four, and received her CPA license. It was a major accomplishment, and something she was very proud of.

Peter asked Emily if she would go out to breakfast with him in the morning. That night she could hardly sleep, thinking about him.

Emily believed she would see Peter again, after meeting him at Stowe. After all, Snow *promised* her she would. But a small part of her questioned the possibility of that really happening. Now that it had happened, it was almost too much to grasp.

But it was a good thing and she was very excited about the days ahead.

The next morning Peter picked her up and drove her to a quaint little diner for breakfast.

Emily ordered scrambled eggs and toast.
Peter ordered two eggs over easy with toast.
As they sat across from each other at the
table, Peter shook his head in disbelief. He
couldn't believe Emily was actually sitting
in front of him.

Since he bumped into her at Stowe, there
wasn't a day that went by, that he hadn't
thought of her. And on top of that, she was
his mother's neighbor. How incredible was
that?

His mother had told him so many times on
the phone, "you've got to meet Emily, she's
perfect for you."

Mother knows best, thought Peter, no, its
father knows best. Well, either way, the
best was yet to come.

After breakfast they went to the hospital to
pick up Vivian. When they entered her
hospital room, she was already dressed and
ready to leave.

The doctor recommended that she start
going to a diabetes specialist, but in the
meantime, gave her a sample diet to follow.

All the way home the three of them laughed. Nana was shocked that Dwight was the one Emily met at Stowe.

"Its fate," said Nana, "You young people had better not take this lightly. Life has enough challenges without ignoring a gift placed right in front of you. You both need to carpe diem, seize the day, make the most of everyday. I wish I could turn back the clock on my own life. I would cherish so many days that I took for granted."

"For starters," said Nana, "you are both going out tonight on a dinner date, and I'm paying for it. Go to the Parker House, it's a nice romantic restaurant."

Emily and Peter were speechless. Yes they liked each other, but they hadn't talked about it.

Peter looked over to Emily. "Would you like to go out to dinner tonight?"

Emily looked back at Peter. She smiled and said, "I'd like that." Peter smiled back.

They got Nana all settled in, and helped her prepare lunch.

As Emily and Peter sat at the kitchen table, flirtatious looks went back and forth.

Although they hadn't talked about their inner feelings with each other, they just knew there was a real connection.
It was nerve racking and exciting all at the same time.

Emily was so awestruck with Peter, she had totally forgotten about Harry. The Detective couldn't find anything on him. Nonetheless Emily was on cloud nine, not Harry or anyone else could distract her now.

Emily was glad to find out that Peter was no longer engaged. He had broken off the engagement the week before he met Emily at the Rusty Nail. Nana was thrilled with the news. She never liked the girl. Emily was even more thrilled, since she had no intentions of dating an engaged man.

It's like Snow always told Emily, timing. Snow told her Mr. Right would come into her life at just the right time. Here he had broken off his engagement, and a week later met Emily. He went to Stowe to get away, and met her totally unexpectedly.

Emily went home to change for dinner. She was so excited. When she got home, she listened to a message from Snow on her answering machine.

"Have a great time tonight. Nana called and told me about your hot date. You have no idea how happy Kevin and I are for you. We are thrilled, and we love Peter, he seems really terrific. We love you Ebe!"

Emily smiled. "Yes, finally Mr. Right."

Emily and Peter had a 6:30 reservation at The Parker House. The restaurant, and Bed & Breakfast, was in a beautiful brick Victorian building with a charming front porch.

As they entered the front door, Adam, the owner, a dashing handsome man, warmly greeted them. He seated them in the dining room with the fireplace.

Peter ordered a bottle of Meursault. Nana had already told him it was Emily's favorite. Peter held up his glass and made a toast to Emily, "To fate, thank you for bringing me at this time, to this place." Emily tapped his glass. "To fate."

Emily ordered a salad and Peter ordered Oven Roasted Asparagus topped with Brie. For dinner, they both ordered the Panko Crusted Wild King Salmon topped with Strawberry-fennel Chutney.

Peter and Emily spent the night laughing. Everything they said was right. As they talked to each other, it was as if no one else was in the restaurant.

They talked about Nana, about work and even their past marriages.

It turns out that Peter was a CEO for a Fortune 500 company, which of course was on the New York stock exchange.

Emily told Peter how hard the CPA exams were and how hard it was to study for them.

They ordered Crème Brule for dessert. Emily said it was the best she ever had.

Alexandra, the master chef and also Adam's wife, always makes the most delicious food.

She came out to their table to say hello, and since she knew Nana, offered them a free after dinner drink.

At a quarter to twelve they finally left to go home. They could have stayed there all night , they were having such a good time. Neither one of them could ever remember having so much fun.

Peter mentioned on their way home, that he had never gone on a horse drawn sleigh ride, and wondered if there was a place locally to do that.

Emily knew of a place in South Woodstock.

"Great," said Peter, "let's do that tomorrow."

CHAPTER EIGHTEEN

The next morning Emily went to Nana's. Peter told them he was making breakfast. Emily liked it when a man cooks.

Peter made apple pancakes and Vermont bacon. He also made a large pot of Vermont flavored coffee.

"What are you two lovebirds doing today?" asked Nana. Peter and Emily looked at each other and smiled.

"We're going for a sleigh ride in South Woodstock."

"Excellent," said Nana, "How romantic!"

"Mother?" asked Dwight, "What are you doing today?"

Nana answered, "I've decided to write a book."

Peter and Emily looked at Nana in disbelief. "A book?" asked Dwight. "Yes dear, a book. Emily gave me the idea. I have a lot to tell, since I've been married four times, I'm naming it *"FOUR I DO'S"*."

"I love it," said Emily, "What a perfect name. How did you come up with it?"

"I woke up this morning and it popped into my mind. It will give me something to do, besides exercising, which I still plan to do."

"I'm starting the book this morning, right after you kids leave."

"How will you write it Nana?" asked Emily.

"Oh that's the easy part," said Nana. "I already have a word processing program on my computer, which corrects as you type. And I also have a professional program which turns your finished manuscript into a computer file for the publisher."

Dwight stood there looking at his mother in amazement. "Mother, where did you learn all this?"

Vivian looked at her son. "Do you think because I'm 75, I'm out of the loop?"

"No mother," answered Dwight, "it's just that you surprise me."
"Good," said Vivian.

Nana turned to Emily, "Remember that dear, always surprise them, keep them guessing. Men get bored with predictable women."

"I figured if Grandma Moses started her career at age 76, then I certainly can start mine at 75." Emily laughed.

CHAPTER NINETEEN

Nana started typing her book as soon as they left. She was laughing and crying through every page.

If she questioned her wording or spelling, she would right click on her mouse for spell check or the Thesaurus.

At lunch time she checked on line for bar-coding (her ISBN number for register scanning) and for copywriting.

"Wow," thought Nana, "everything is so easy nowadays." She ordered her bar-code online and printed out her copyright registration form.

While Emily and Dwight were out having fun, Nana wrote 25 pages. She couldn't wait for them to get back home so she could read it to them.

Nana started writing about her childhood. She was born in 1932, three years after the Wall Street Crash of 1929. That was when people jumped off buildings. Some regard it as the start of the Great Depression.

It was a time when people were thrifty, they had no choice. Nana read somewhere that although it was difficult times, women still bought their lipstick.

As Vivian wrote about those early days, she thought how different it was now. There was no wasting back then, and now we tend to discard things so easily, even our marriages.

When Emily and Dwight came home, they were so surprised to hear of Nana's accomplishment.

Dwight made three hot chocolates , one was a sugar free for Nana. They sat in the living room and Vivian read them what she wrote. Nana and Emily were crying. Dwight looked at his mother and said, "I had no idea Grandmother and Grandfather went through such hardships. I'm so glad you are writing this down. It looks as though I'll have a wonderful treasure of your life."

Nana looked over to Dwight and smiled.

"Mother," said Dwight, "Emily and I would like you to join us for dinner tonight. We thought we'd go to the Woodstock Inn. We can celebrate the start your new book."

CHAPTER TWENTY

During the following weeks, Emily and Peter constantly talked with each other on the phone.

Peter had to get back to work. Being a CEO carried huge responsibilities, but he was good at what he did. He had been a CEO for five years. His life had been very stressful.

Meeting Emily had altered his thinking and priorities. Every weekend he went back to Vermont to see her.

They made an attractive couple, just as his mother said they would. They grew so close over the past few weeks, that when one of them started to speak, the other was thinking the same thought.

Emily had never been so happy. She walked around with a smile on her face all the time. When she heard the phone ring, she would run to it, hoping it was Peter, and most often it was. She was literally on cloud nine.

The following week was Valentines Day. Nana told them they should go somewhere for the weekend.

Peter suggested they go to the "Trapp Family Lodge." It was totally appropriate that they celebrate in the town where they met. Emily called Snow and told her all about their plans.

"This will be the first time we'll be alone," said Emily, "I'm a little scared. We've kissed a few times, but we've never gone wild. I've dreamed about our first intimate time together, but I'm still afraid."

"Why are you afraid?" asked Snow.

"It's been a year and a half since I've been with a man. I'm in love with Peter, I want to please him."

"I wouldn't worry about it," said Snow, "I know he loves you and just being with you will satisfy all his needs. I was afraid with Kevin, but things were better than I could have imagined. True love makes sex better. Don't worry , I'm sure it will be heaven for both of you."

"Promise?" asked Emily. "Promise," said Snow, "and lately my promises have proven well."

CHAPTER TWENTY-ONE

Emily and Peter arrived at the *Trapp Family Lodge* around noon. It was so beautiful on the mountain. There had been a snow storm the night before, so fresh snow covered all the roofs and trees. It looked magical. It was a winter wonderland.

It was a pleasure to stay at the Lodge because the service was so good and everyone was so helpful. Peter had reserved the most deluxe suite for them.

As they entered their room, a large bouquet of roses sat on the dresser. They were all different colors; white, red, yellow, pink, coral and even lilac. Emily never saw such an elaborate mixed bouquet before. Peter told her to open the card.

"You've captured my heart. I've waited all my life for you. I love you, Peter."

Emily had tears in her eyes. Peter walked over to her. He wrapped his arms around her and kissed her passionately on her lips.

Emily looked into Peter's eyes. "I love you, too."

They bundled up and went for a sleigh ride. Just as the horse started to pull them through the snow, snowflakes started falling. It was like a Christmas movie. It was so romantic.

Emily sat so close to Peter, that if she sat any closer, she would be on the other side of him. He wrapped his arm around her shoulders and kissed her on her cheek. "You're my little Snow Angel," said Peter. Emily smiled back.

They rode through fields and tree lined paths. It was so wonderful.

When they got back to the Lodge they decided to take a walk in town. As they walked down Main Street they saw a poster that read: "Make your own Candy Canes - December through February".

They walked inside and saw a woman stretching large taffy like pieces onto a cookie sheet. It was cream colored but as it cooled it became white. She mixed it with some red sheets of the same mixture. This caused the scent of peppermint to fill the room, clearing everyone's sinuses.

She then rolled them together and started to pull the roll until it got very thin. Everyone got a section to work with.

Peter made a heart out of his and Emily made a typical candy cane. They placed their candy in clear cellophane bags and tied them with red ribbons.

The woman then handed everyone peppermint hot chocolate as they left. As they continued to walk down the street they came across another poster that read: "Make your own Gingerbread House". Of course they went in and made a house together.

They continued to walk around town and soon came to the Ferro Jewelry Store. Peter held the door as Emily hesitated to walk in.

As they walked over to the counter Peter looked at Emily, "pick out any ring you want. …just say you'll marry me."

Emily looked at Peter. She couldn't believe what she was hearing.

"Will you marry me? asked Peter, "If you say yes, I'll spend the rest of my life making you happy."

Emily looked at Peter. "Yes…Yes."
Emily was drawn to one ring, the Snowflake
diamond, the same ring Snow has. Kevin
had bought Snow's ring at NT Ferro in
Woodstock.

"Are you sure you want the same one?"
asked Peter.

"Yes," replied Emily, "I told Snow when
she got engaged that I wanted the same ring
when I found Mr.Right."

She said to me, "Then we'll be sisters, not
just friends."

Bryan Ferro, the Jeweler, took the ring out
of the case and handed it to Peter. Peter
looked at Emily and reached over to hold
her hand. "You are the love of my life."

Peter placed the ring on her finger. Emily
was surprised to find it fit perfectly.
"It's a sign," said Emily.

As soon as they left the store Emily called
Snow on her cell phone. Then she called
Vivian, and Dwight told his mother the good
news. "It's about time," said Nana, "let me
talk to the bride."

"I told you my son was perfect for you."

"You were right Nana, you were right.
How are you doing and how is your book
coming along?" asked Emily.

"I'm on page 96 and I'm crying all the time
as I hash up old memories."

"That's so wonderful," said Emily, "I'm so
proud of you. You may have to write
another book at this speed."

Nana laughed.

"Well congratulations Dear, I couldn't ask
for a better daughter in-law."

CHAPTER TWENTY-TWO

Emily was so happy. She totally forgot about Harry. She had checked her email before she went to Stowe. No emails from Harry. That was good.

Ever since the night Nana went to the hospital, there were no more emails from Harry, and Emily wasn't worried about it either. Peter was her main thought now, and nothing else mattered.

That night Peter took Emily to the best restaurant in Stowe. As they entered the restaurant, Emily could see a beautifully set table for two.

A red rose lay across her place setting and a bottle of Dom Perignon was on ice.

All Emily could think, was *"somewhere in my youth or childhood, I must have done something good!"*

It was a dream comes true, and if it was a dream, she didn't want to wake up.

Peter held up his champagne glass to make a toast. "I promise you this night, that I will love you forever." Emily tapped his glass, "Forever."

They ordered Mussels cooked in wine for their appetizer, and Roasted Duck for their main entree.

During their meal they talked about Snow and Kevin, Nana, and plans for their wedding.

"Of course my mother will fly out," said Emily, "and my three brothers. Snow will be my maid of honor."

"I have some more news to tell you," said Peter, "I resigned from my company. I have enough money in stocks and IRA's and Roth's and a retirement plan that will cover us for the rest of our lives. If you decide to stop working, I would be thrilled, but I know you love accounting and you just achieved your CPA, so whatever makes you happy, will make me happy too."

"As a matter of fact," said Peter, "if you would like to open your own CPA firm in Woodstock or Quechee, I will buy a building for you as a wedding gift."

Emily was speechless.

For dessert they had heart shaped chocolate molten cakes with vanilla ice cream and drizzled raspberry sauce.

During dinner they flirted shamelessly, but didn't care. They had to make up for lost time, and wanted the whole world to know they loved each other.

On the way back up the mountain to the Lodge, Peter suggested they have a nightcap at the Rusty Nail, since that was where they met.

They parked and walked into the bar. Kate was there. They shared their good news with her and she was so happy for them. Kate told them she hadn't seen Harry since the last time they were in. The place was packed so they only had one drink and went back to the Lodge.

When they opened the door to their suite, a beautiful fire was burning in the fireplace and their bed sheets were turned down. Wrapped chocolates were placed on their pillows.

Peter helped Emily take off her coat. He then placed his arms around her and kissed her passionately on her lips and lightly licked her ear lobe. Peter held her hand, leading her to the bed. Emily had butterflies in her stomach.

"I have a surprise for you, *Snow Angel*."

"I want to give you a special massage. I brought a wonderful oil to massage you with." Emily liked the idea.

Peter unzipped her dress. Emily slowly dropped it to the floor. She had no underwear on. She was completely naked under her dress.

Peter was at full attention as he looked at her breasts and sandy blonde sex mound. He wanted to take her right then. He had been thinking about her being naked ever since they met at the Rusty Nail.

He leaned down to kiss and suck her breasts. Emily moaned. She was no longer afraid. Emily had become sexually aroused when she dropped her dress to the floor.

"If I had known you weren't wearing underwear," said Peter, "I would have skipped dinner."

Emily laughed.

She noticed Peter's bulging manhood behind his zipper and reached down to his belt buckle and undid it. She then unzippered his pants and pulled them to the floor.

His manhood was huge. She quickly put him in her mouth, letting his sex spear go down her throat. Peter moaned loudly. She sucked him good.

Emily glanced up at him, while his spear was in her mouth. It was a picture men dream of. With her mouth full, she could barely say, "I love you."

Peter pulled her up to his lips, "How I love you," and kissed her hard. His sex spear went right between her thighs and she tightened them.

Peter looked at Emily, "Darling, lay on the bed, I want to massage you."

Emily laid flat on her stomach with her arms folded under her head. Peter quickly took off his shirt and grabbed the massage oil.

He climbed up on top of her with his manhood grouping rubbing against her love cheeks.

Just feeling him on her made her wild. He slowly sprinkled drops of oil on her back. He gently rubbed it into her skin. It was so wonderful and it felt so good. He then moved down toward her feet, dragging his manhood along her legs as he sprinkled more oil. Emily moaned.

Peter got up and Emily rolled over. He lowered his head to her sandy mound. He gently licked her with the tip of his tongue, sending unbelievable sensations through out her body. She started to move her body as if he were already in her. It turned him on in a way no woman had done before.

Emily called out his name. "Oh Peter, yes, yes....Peter...Peter." Emily soon cried out. She had been fully pleasured.

Peter got excited hearing his name called out. He wanted to force his sex spear in her, he couldn't wait any longer. Emily reached down and grabbed his spear. She placed it in her mouth sucking it wildly.

Peter screamed out. "Ohh…Ohh…Ohhh…."
He could no longer hold back. He swiftly
forced his bulging sex spear into her warm
wet walls.

That feeling, thought Emily, was oh so
good, feeling him enter her sugar walls,
pushing her open.

He filled her completely. He was a perfect
fit. Peter slid his spear in and out. They
moaned madly.

He relentlessly pushed in and out. It felt so
warm, wet and good. Neither one of them
wanted to stop.

Emily cried out his name. Peter looked
down at her, watching his spear move in and
out. Emily wanted more, and so he gave it
to her.

He reached down to her love mounds
sucking them both. Emily moaned loudly.
Soon Peter cried out.

He slowly laid down on Emily's sweaty
warm body. He kissed her lighty.

"If I had known it was going to be this good, I would have gone to your house instead of my mothers."

Emily laughed. "And I was afraid I'd disappoint you."

Peter looked at her. "Are you kidding? This is the best sex I've ever had. If I hadn't already asked you to marry me, I certainly would now." Emily smiled.

CHAPTER TWENTY-THREE

The next morning Emily woke up with Peter's arms wrapped around her. It was heaven.

They made love again and then dressed to go eat breakfast.

They glowed. Their love was so strong that it showed.

They had planned to go skiing after breakfast, but instead went back to the suite for more sex, staying there for the remainder of the day.

Sunday morning they skied until lunchtime and then headed home.

As soon as they got back, they went over to Nana's. Peter decided to cook a pork tenderloin marinated in balsamic vinegar, rosemary, garlic, red wine and extra virgin olive oil. He served roasted vegetables with the pork.

After dinner, Snow and Kevin drove over to Nana's with a bottle of Dom Perignon to celebrate Emily and Peter's engagement.

They spent hours laughing and sharing stories. Snow was so glad that Emily chose the same engagement ring she had. As Snow looked at Emily's ring, she turned to her and said, "Sisters." Emily smiled.

Nana read a few excerpts from her book, leaving Emily and Snow in tears.

"Nana," said Emily, "I had no idea you went through such hard times growing up." Nana smiled at Emily and Snow.

"Thank God," said Nana, "that you don't know ahead of time. One day at a time was all I could handle. In spite of it all, good things did happen, like Dwight." Emily looked at Peter and smiled.

That night Peter stayed at Emily's. The sex just kept getting better.

The next morning Peter got out of bed to go to the bathroom. As he passed Emily's dresser, he noticed a picture of a man. He looked back at Emily and asked, "Where did you get this picture?"

Emily looked at Peter. "That's Daddy."

Peter looked at the picture then back at Emily. "He's my father too."

Emily sat straight up in her bed. "What?"

"Well, stepfather, I should say."

"Stepfather?" asked Emily.

Emily and Peter got dressed and walked over to Nana's. When Nana opened her door she saw two gloomy faces. "What? What's wrong?" They went inside and sat down.

Nana and Emily shared everything they remembered about Emily's father.

"I thought he was a traveling salesman," said Nana, "I had no idea. I'm so sorry dear."

Emily called her mother, Katherine, who arrived on the next flight to Vermont. By Monday night Emily's mother was in Quechee.

Emily and her mother walked over to Nana's. At first the conversation between them was cool but within a half an hour they were laughing with each other. At times they cried, but mostly laughed.

To their surprise they had a lot in common.

In the days that followed, they became **good** friends. Katherine even gave Vivian permission to mention her in her book.

Emily's mother sold her house in Ohio and bought a house that was for sale on Emily's street. She and Vivian became best friends and exercised together regularly.

Emily and Peter couldn't wait for spring, so they married on March 5th. They got married at the Woodstock Inn. It was a small wedding, just fifteen people. The wedding favors were little bow tied boxes of French chocolate from the Wm Winand Chocolatier in Woodstock. Emily's brothers stayed at The Charleston House. They were good friends with Willa and Dixi, the owners, and loved their special breakfast.

Peter moved in with Emily and bought her a small building in Quechee as a wedding gift, where she opened her own CPA office.

Snow, Emily, Kevin and Peter spent most of their weekends together and never heard from Harry again. Kevin shared recipes with Peter and they all lived "*Happily Ever After*" just like in the books and movies, in the beautiful and peaceful State of Vermont.

ABOUT THE AUTHOR

Dorothea Zsenai Mongulla is a Vermont resident and Real Estate Broker in Woodstock, Vermont. She is married to Michael and has two daughters, Jennifer and Abigail. She has a Black cat named Gizmo. Dorothea has a Great love for the State of Vermont and reflects that in her writings.

Available at: Amazon.com
Also available from the author at:
trueloveinvermont@verizon.net

Dorothea's first book was:
True Love In Vermont

Cover designed by:
Jon-Mikel Gates, Graphic Designer at Anything Printed Taftsville, VT
802-457-3414

Photographer: Dorothea Mongulla
Front Cover: Bennington, VT
Back Cover: Stowe, VT